No Time for Mother's Day

WRITTEN BY

Laurie Halse Anderson

ILLUSTRATED BY

Dorothy Donohue

Albert Whitman & Company

Morton Grove, Illinois

Library of Congress Cataloging-in-Publication Data
Anderson, Laurie Halse.
No time for Mother's Day / by Laurie Halse Anderson ;
illustrated by Dorothy Donohue.
p. cm.
Summary: Although it takes her some time, Charity thinks
of the perfect Mother's Day gift for her busy mother.
ISBN 0-8075-4955-X
[1. Mother's Day—Fiction. 2. Gifts—Fiction.]
I. Donohue, Dorothy, ill. II. Title.
PZ7.A54385No   1999
[E]—dc21
98-33757
CIP AC

Published in 1999 by Albert Whitman & Company,
6340 Oakton Street, Morton Grove, Illinois 60053-2723.
Published simultaneously in Canada by General Publishing, Limited, Toronto.
Printed in the United States of America.
10 9 8 7 6 5 4 3 2

The illustrations are rendered in pen and ink, colored pencil, and watercolors.
The text is set in Cushing Book.
The design is by Scott Piehl.

"Sunday will be Mother's Day," Ms. Evans reminded her class. "It's time to make cards for your mothers."

Charity Chatfield sat up straight in her chair. Only two days?
It couldn't be, she thought.

"I bought my mother two gallons of chocolate-chip ice cream," said Megan.

"We're going to take my mom to the movies," said Emma.

Charity peeled the paper off her crayon. "I don't know what to give Mom," she mumbled.

"Moms can be tricky," said Jason. "Give her a velociraptor. She'll love that."

"You'd better decide fast," added Megan. "You don't have much time."

Saturday morning was frantic as usual. The telephone rang, the toaster buzzed, and the dishwasher made a funny noise. Mom answered the phone, rescued the toast, emptied the dishwasher, and checked the clock. The microwave chirped. The timer beeped.

Charity buttered her toast. She was trying to figure out a good present. Only twenty-four hours left.

"Time to get going," Mom said. "Hop in the car, honey. I'll grab the dog."

"Your office sent a fax!" called Dad.
"I'll have to read it later," said Mom.

Mom could use five more hands, thought Charity.
That would really help her.

Mom and Charity raced through
their errands.
The video store,
the library,
and the bank. Hurry, scurry.
The post office,

the doughnut shop,

and the dry cleaners.

Hurry, hurry, scurry.

The vet, the shoe store,

the hardware store.

Hurry, hurry, scurry, scurry!

Finally, the grocery store.

It was jammed with people. Babies cried. Carts crashed. Charity and her mother pushed up one aisle and down the next.

Mom's beeper bleeped in Frozen Foods. She called her office while stacking waffles in the cart.

Mom could use five more hands and another pair of legs, Charity thought.

Mom sighed. "I have to go to work. Your father is taking you to the mall with Fred."

Charity groaned. "Not Fred!" she said.

At the mall, Cousin Fred pulled out a list.

"My mommy wrote down exactly what she wants. She gave me money," he bragged. "Follow me."

Fred bought Aunt Imogene flashy earrings and a bracelet.

Charity and Dad looked at the jewelry. It wasn't Mom's style.

Fred bought Aunt Imogene a smelly candle, stinky perfume, and peculiar purple bubble bath.

Charity and Dad held their breath. Mom didn't like things that smelled.

"We can't stop now," said Fred. "I've just started."

Charity and Dad couldn't find anything.
"Buy her flowers," suggested Fred.
"Flowers make her sneeze," said Dad.
"Candy?" tried Fred.
"She never eats it," said Charity.
"How about a velociraptor?"

Charity crossed her arms. "You are no help," she said.

"Maybe we could *do* something for her," Dad said. "I could paint the kitchen."

"But what can *I* do?" asked Charity.

"She loves your pictures," said Dad. "Why don't you draw her one?"

That night, Charity tried drawing.
"Your mom doesn't need another picture," said Fred.
"She already has a million of them."

Charity's stomach flipped. "Be quiet," she said. "I only have twelve hours left!"

"You're sunk," said Fred with a grin.

"Time for Fred to go home!" Dad called. "Time for bed!"

Charity woke up when the grandfather clock bonged twelve times. It was midnight. Eight hours left, and she still didn't have a present!

She woke up again when the clock bonged once. One o'clock.

She counted the minutes. 1:01. 1:02.
An idea rang in Charity's head as loud as an alarm. The perfect Mother's Day present!

Mother's Day began when Aunt Imogene and Fred burst through the door.

"IT'S MOTHER'S DAY!" shouted Aunt Imogene.
"WAKE UP!"

Dad started pancakes while Aunt Imogene ripped the wrapping paper off her boxes.

"OH, MY GOODNESS, WHAT A SURPRISE!" she squealed. "GIVE MUMMY A KISS, FREDDY-TEDDIE, THEN HAND ME ANOTHER BOX."

When Aunt Imogene had opened all of her presents, Charity
looked at Mom.

"Now it's *your* turn," Charity said.

Dad brought in the paint cans. "I'm going to repaint the kitchen for you," he said.

"THAT'S NOT A PRESENT," protested Aunt Imogene.

"It's a wonderful present," said Mom. "Just what I want."

"And now it's time for *my* present," said Charity.

She put her finger to her lips. "Shhhh!"
The whole family stopped.
"Do you hear that?" asked Charity.
"Hear what?" asked Mom.
Charity grinned. "It's your present," she explained.

"A whole day of peace and quiet. I unplugged the little clocks and stopped the big ones. Everything that beeps or bleeps or buzzes is turned off. Your Mother's Day present is time to do whatever you want. Just for fun."

The family stood still, listening to the wonderful silence.
Mom sighed happily. "Ahhhh. It's the perfect present. It's
exactly what I wanted the most." She leaned forward. "But
I *do* know what time it is."

"You do?" asked Charity.

"It's time for a hug!"